The BIG BAD WOLF Goes on Vacation

The BIG BAD WOLF
Goes on Vacation

DELPHINE PERRET

STERLING CHILDREN'S BOOKS
New York

An Imprint of Sterling Publishing
387 Park Avenue South
New York, NY 10016

STERLING CHILDREN'S BOOKS
and the distinctive Sterling Children's Books logo are trademarks of Sterling Publishing Co., Inc.

The artwork for this book was created using pencil on white paper, and was then colored digitally for the English language edition.
Designed by Richard Amari

ISBN 978-1-4027-8633-4

Library of Congress Cataloging-in-Publication Data

Perret, Delphine.
  [Moi le loup et les vacances avec Pepe. English]
  The Big Bad Wolf goes on vacation / Delphine Perret.
       p. cm.
  Summary: When Bernard, the Big Bad Wolf, joins Louis and his grandfather on their annual trip to the beach, getting there is half the fun.
  ISBN 978-1-4027-8633-4 [1. Wolves--Fiction. 2. Vacations--Fiction. 3. Grandfathers--Fiction. 4. Characters in literature--Fiction. 5. Humorous stories.] I. Title.
  PZ7.P4328Bim 2013
  [E]--dc23

                                                            2012009933

Distributed in Canada by Sterling Publishing c/o Canadian Manda Group, 165 Dufferin Street Toronto, Ontario, Canada M6K 3H6
Distributed in the United Kingdom by GMC Distribution Services; Castle Place, 166 High Street, Lewes, East Sussex, England BN7 1XU
Distributed in Australia by Capricorn Link (Australia) Pty. Ltd. P.O. Box 704, Windsor, NSW 2756, Australia

For information about custom editions, special sales, and premium and corporate purchases,
please contact Sterling Special Sales at 800-805-5489 or specialsales@sterlingpublishing.com.

Manufactured in China
Lot #:
2 4 6 8 10 9 7 5 3 1
10/12

To my papa.

CHAPTER *1*

Tomorrow is the last day of school.
I can't *wait* for summer vacation to start.

But I still have one more piece
of homework to finish . . .

and it's taking
FOREVER.

Pencil Mustache Champion
of the **World**!

Louis, are you doing
your **homework**?

CHAPTER 2

You'd be distracted, too, if the Big Bad Wolf lived in your closet.
It's not easy keeping him a secret from everyone.

This homework is **hard**.

May I see?

CRUNCH

CRUNCH

CRUNCH

CRUNCH

CRUNCH

Bernard, stop crunching so **LOUD**!

What's wrong?

You're getting crumbs all over my neck!

And now I'm **itchy**!

You want me to leave you alone?

YES.

Too bad . . .

I see you've made a few mistakes on your homework.

Oh, please help me— this is really **important**.

You won't mind a few crumbs?

Not at all.

Okay, you have to add a three there . . .

CRUNCH

CRUNCH

CHAPTER 3

Homework: done. Suitcase: ready!

Grandpa will be here soon to take me to the beach. I can't wait to see the **OCEAN** again.

Ummm...

Can I come, too?

Well, I could ask Grandpa. But you'd have to go incognito. No talking in public.

Deal! Let's go to the beach!

**Wait. What's a beach?
What's an ocean?**

Imagine the bathtub, but
about a billion times bigger!
With seashells! And sand!
And really huge waves!

And **NO** shampoo!
The beach is the
best place in the world.

**Sounds amazing!
So, will you ask
your grandpa if
I can come?**

Okay, but you
have to promise
not to eat him.

You forget that I'm a vegetarian.

A vege-*what*?

"Vegetarian!" It says
right here in the
dictionary: "Someone
who does not eat meat."

Hmmph.

But you love salmon
and sardines!

**Well, as long as
your grandpa
doesn't look like a
sardine, he's safe.**

CHAPTER 4

Finally, my wonderful grandpa arrived.

There's my favorite grandson!

Grandpa!

You ready to go?

I've been ready for *weeks*.

Have fun, Louis! Send us a postcard!

Grandpa?

Would it be okay if I brought a furry friend along to keep us company?

Huh? Oh sure, why not?
You may bring your little
HAMSTER if you like.
He can sit on your lap.

On my lap?

His name is
Bernard.

Boo!

Hello.

I'm the
Big Bad Wolf.

And *I* am the queen
of England.

Really?

No, in fact I'm King Kong. Huh?

BOO! YIKES!

Hee hee. Sorry!
Come on, let's go
to the beach.

?

Your grandpa is really cool,
but I like him better when
he's the queen of England.

CHAPTER 5

Our trip to the beach was off to a good start.

A wolf. He's only *pretending* to be a dog so that he can keep his true identity a secret.

Well, that makes sense...

and he's doing a very convincing job!

CHAPTER 6

Sometimes I forget that Bernard is a very sensitive wolf.

Here's your ticket. You'll pay
at the next toll booth.

Thanks.

What a cute little
doggie you have!

Oh, uh . . . thank you!

What's wrong with him?

That lady hurt his feelings.

He's the **BIG BAD WOLF**, after all.

It's not easy to pretend
to be something else.

Is he usually a
little bit scarier?

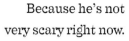

Because he's not
very scary right now.

He works hard at it,
but it's true that he
doesn't eat children
anymore . . .

Mmmm . . .
I could go for a big,
juicy pork chop.

or little pigs.

He doesn't eat meat. He likes chocolate chip cookies, licorice, sardines, ice cream . . .

grated carrots, graham crackers . . .

GRRRRR

Your wolf sounds really *angry* all of a sudden.

GRUMBLE! GGROOOOOWL!!

No, it's just that hearing
about all that great food
has made me very **hungry!**

GRRRR!

CHAPTER 7

It was definitely time to stop for lunch.

Who wants a sandwich?

Me!

Me, too!

I want tomato and mayo.

Or tuna on rye!

Or do you think they'll have sardines with whipped cream?

**Never mind—
I'll just choose
when we go in.**

You can't come in!
You walk on two legs,
and you might forget
not to talk.

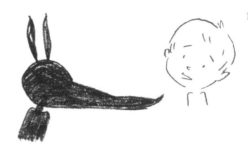

**I am wounded by
your lack of trust.**

There *is* a solution. But
you're not going to like it.

CHAPTER 8

We found an empty park where we could eat our lunch in peace.
We were a great team—just the three of us.

Ha ha! Real cool and mysterious!

Okay, fine. I will wrap up my gum in this paper in a cool and classy way.

At least *I* don't stick *my* gum under a **park bench.**

Hee hee—he's got you there, Louis.

Tattletale!

Anyway, as I was saying before, a wolf is not the same as a dog. The wild is always calling to me. Can you hear it?

It sounds like a poodle.

A poodle?

ARF!

ARF!

ARF!

ARF!

ROAARR!

YIPE!

YIPE!

There's no shame in being mistaken for a dog . . . but it's a LOT more fun to be the Big Bad Wolf!

CHAPTER 9

Every five minutes, Bernard asked, "Are we THERE yet?"

Where did I put
that ticket?

It's a little card.
Have you seen it?

What does it
look like?

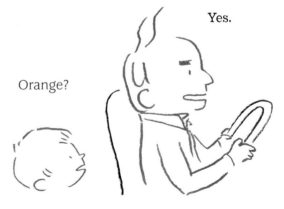

Yes.

Orange?

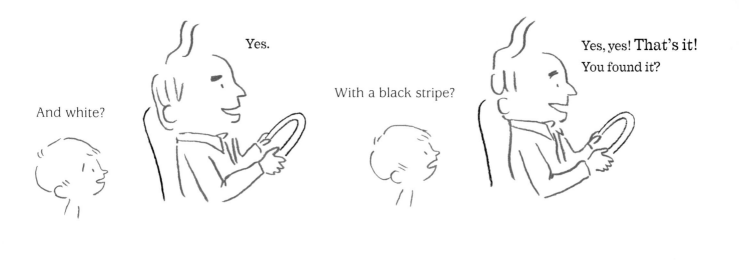

Hello.

CHAPTER *10*

You never know *what* you might see when you're on vacation.

Ah! Smell that fresh country air!
Roll down your windows.

Take some deep breaths—
it's good for you.

A nice change
from the city, eh?

What's wrong?

**I think I just
swallowed a fly.**

We'll have to push them out of the way.

I LOVE cows.

?

Hello, my **big beauty.** You are my **friend!** You are . . .

Mffrrr.

Ewww!

Moo?

He's got style, that wolf!

Get out of here, you band of slugs! We have to get to the beach!

GROWL! Moo! Moo Moo!

GRRRR!

CHAPTER *11*

A wolf, even a friendly one, is still wild at heart.

I have ants in
my pants.

I'll stop here so you
can stretch your legs.

I think I'll run in
those woods.

Are you sure
it's safe?

Don't you worry—
the wild world knows me!

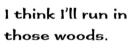

While I'm in there, I'll hunt down a snack for us, too.

?

Grrrr!

Does Bernard know how to hunt?

Only if the hunt involves a cookie jar or a refrigerator.

What's taking so long? Do you think he's okay?

I'm sure he's fine.

But what if something hunts *him*? What if he gets attacked by a bear? Or a **WILD BOAR?** Or a **MOUNTAIN LION?!**

Or a skunk!

Ew. If a skunk sprays him, I'm not sharing my seat!

Ah! Here he comes.

What's that he's carrying?

I found us some chocolate chip cookies.

In the **forest**??

No, silly. On the other side of the trees there's a **vending machine!**

CHAPTER 12

When we were tired of sitting, and sick of counting cars, and the seats were full of cookie crumbs . . . that's when we finally arrived.

We'll soon be able
to see the ocean—

Oh no, I saw it right away.

Not true—
it was me.

I'm sure I shouted first.

Definitely not—
I said it before you.

**Maybe that's what YOU
heard, but my wolf ears
are more finely tuned.**

I know very well
I spoke up at least
a second before you.

Hey, you two, here is the ocean!

Wow! It's really big. But I am a cool and mysterious wolf, and I will contain my excitement.

Me, too. I'm not a little kid anymore, so I won't race into the water like last summer.

I'm not really the type to yell, "Me, first!"

Me neither . . . unlike *you* a little while ago.

I know how to keep my cool.

So do I.

Hee hee!

I'm going to be the first one to put my toes in the water!

WHOOSH!

A vacation without a wolf is like a beach without seashells.